BROKEN HEART

Horror Fiction

notionpress.com

BROKEN HEART

Horror Fiction

"I will hunt down and kill each one of you!"

JIVAN

notionpress.com

Notion Press

5 Muthu Kalathy Street, Triplicane,

Chennai - 600 005

First Published by Notion Press 2014

ISBN: 978-93-84381-32-5

Short synopsis

A young married couple Ajay and Maya from New Delhi decides to spend their honeymoon at hill resort Kodaikanal in Tamil Nadu. Near the suicide point at about 8.30 P.M. in the pouring rain Ajay was brutally beaten to death and Maya gets gang raped and murdered. They burnt the body of Ajay and Maya so that there is no evidence. Only Ajay alone comes back to life! Out of ten million people in Chennai city Ajay will have to hunt down and kill each one of the perpetrators of crime in a gruesome manner. The special appearance, character and special power given to Ajay make this fiction interesting and unique.

Visit my Blog for fictions and articles.
http://jivadax.blogspot.in

Author's Note

This fiction is the creation of my imagination. And person living or dead is purely coincidence. Characters, people, groups, organizations, companies, and agencies described in this novel are either the work of the author's imagination; or, if real, are used fictitiously; without any real intent to describe their actual behavior or conduct.

All places, locations, and buildings described in this novel are real, and descriptions of such are accurate to the best of the author's knowledge.

The author of this novel makes no ownership claim to the documents, publications, books, and songs mentioned or cited in the novel, which are the exclusive property of their respective writers. Quotations or lyrics there from are accurate and are quoted correctly to the best of the author's ability.

Most of the Technologies mentioned in this novel exists some of the future technology used in this fiction are my imagination.

Author of Broken Heart

T.M. Jivan Lal

Broken Heart

(Horror)

Author-Jivan

Our happy family consists of my dad, mom and me. We had our own house in vadapani -Chennai. My dad was working for a north Indian company in Chennai. He was very strict when it comes to studies and disciplines.

After completing my studies as a software engineer I had finished MBA. Even though I got a job offer from Bombay and Delhi my parents wants me to get a job here in Chennai. They do not want me to work in faraway place. My father got promoted and transferred to New Delhi. We rented our house in vadapalani and moved to New Delhi.

I had no friends in New Delhi. I started applying for jobs. My mother was free and frank. She even gets along with perfect strangers. One day after purchasing vegetables from local market she returned home with a middle aged woman and her young daughter. I was in my room going through ethical hacking.

Mummy... "Ajay, come here. I will introduce you to our neighbor".

I came out of my room saw a woman around forty eight years and her young daughter were sitting in our visiting room. I just wished them and sat on the opposite chair.

Maa.. 'Ajay, This is Sheila aunty and her daughter Maya. They are staying in our neighborhood. Just four blocks away from our house on Block L-23. Ajay, you talk with them, I will make coffee for all of us.. ..'

Sheila aunty asked about my studies and future plans. After replying to aunty I asked about Maya. After completing her MBA in HRD she is working for an MNC. her hobby includes writing poems! She must be a romantic creature. Even though she was well groomed she wore traditional dress like Shalwar and kurtha.

Maa brought coffee and samosa with chattini. After coffee and samusa my mother and aunty went into the kitchen. 'We' spoke for some more time... and I found 'we' had lots of things in common.

Maya's mother came back after about twenty minutes and she invited our family for next Sunday lunch at their house and both of them left for their home.

On Sunday our family went to Maya's house and had lunch. Her father was a retired gazetted officer. My dad became his best friend. They found common interest like politics,spiritualism, morning walk which is part of old people.

After about three months I got job in a software company. The pay was good. Since I was posted in New Delhi my parents told me to join for work. After getting first month salary I invited Maya's family for lunch at Hyat Regency. We all had buffet lunch. Food and their service were really good.

It seems the Maya's family had approved óur' friendship. We usually meet after office hours at the near by coffee shop. She was a nice girl with clean habits. She wants someone to approve her poems. She can scribble down poems in a jiffy!. Once she wrote a few verses while having coffee at the coffee shop. Her poems are very simple. You need not read between the lines to understand the meaning of her poems. Her poems are all about love, romance, sentimental values...nothing about intimacy or erotic. Her poems are just like her, simple and down to earth. I likes her poems.

Sometimes we both went for movie with our parents permission. When good family movie runs at the theater we took our parents for moive. Everything seems perfect until one late night around 1.30 am. ...

As usual my father after watching 9.30 news he went to sleep. I was fast asleep in the adjacent room. My father felt uneasy pain on his chest. He got out of bed and asked my mother to lay mat on the floor. He reached for Lord Murugan's photo to pray. Shooting pain on his chest brought him to the floor.

My mother came rushing into my room. Her fanatic calls woke me up. Ájay', your dad is having severe chest pain'. I checked the time. It is my habit whenever I woke up in the middle of the night I check the time. It was 1.35 Am. Immediately I rushed to my parent's room. Father was writhing in pain, he was holding on to his chest. I could see sever pain on his face. I gave him first aid. Artificial respiration. Nothing seems to work. My father did not respond to me. Suddenly his body collapsed. I took the telescope and checked for his heartbeat. Nil. It was 1.38 Am. I knew everything was over May be doctor can revive his heartbeat. My mother started wailing.

Ii called our next door neighbor. Those aged couples came to our house and told me to take dad to the nearest hospital. I said o.k and asked them to look after my mother. I took my bike and went to Maya's house. Her father opened the door for me. I told him what had happened. He then told his wife and Maya to go to my house. Maya and her mother stayed with my mother. Maya's father came with me to the city hospital in my bike. We came back with an ambulance and took my dad back to the hospital. Doctor placed two electrical prods on my father's chest, even after giving electrical pulse charge three times there was no response form my father. The Doctor tried their

best to bring back my father. ..... After some time I receive medical report. 'Brought dead'! We took my father's body back to my home, for me and my mother life seems to come to an end.

Next day on funeral people in the colony came to pay their last respect for my father. At 4p.m we decided to take my father's body for crimination. I lit my father's pyre. ....

After the death of family head we are not supposed to cook food for one week as per our religious custom. Maya's mother prepared food for us…three times per day…for a week. Believe me, very few people in this world will do it for others. We also had to observe fourteen days mourning as per our custom.

After one year.

Maya's parents spoke to my mother about my marriage. Even though they are north Indians they had no problem accepting me as their son in law. But my mother wants our horoscopes to be checked with astrologer. Ten out of eight points matched. My mother was happy. In a simple ceremony I and Maya got married.

After the death of my father my mother was devastated. Maya was a very sensible woman she understood me and my mother. We do not have to ask anything to her, she took care of everything. I really loved her so much. She was charming, intelligent and sensible. It is hard to find someone like her. I was truly blessed.

After marriage I want to take Maya to Chennai. We took permission from our parents and took flight to Chennai. We spent two days on shopping, visiting temples and places of interest in and around Chennai city.

I told Maya we spent some days at kodikanal. I had been to Kodai Kanal with my parents when I was doing

my high school. It is a beautiful hilltop resort. There is a boat club, botanical garden, waterfalls, devils peak made of rocky mountains and caves.....

After spending two days in Chennai we took flight to Madurai. From there we took deluxe bus to Kodaikanal. Next day early morning we arrived at Kodaikanal. We stayed there in a three star hotel next to the lake called Lake View. After taking rest for a few hours we took bath and got dressed up and went to the main restaurant. After breakfast we went for boating. We took rowing boat and went around the lake for about two hours. We also visited botanical garden. We took lots of photographs and returned to our hotel and had our lunch.

In the afternoon we took a taxi and visited devils peak, water fall and went all the way to Palani temple and came back to our room at about 4.30 PM. We had our coffee and snacks and returned to our room and relaxed for some more time.

It was the November month, end of the rainy season. At about six p.m. We went to the reception. The manager greeted both of us. I informed him that we are going for an evening walk. He looked at the sky and told me since it was the end of rainy season some time there will be unexpected rain in hill stations. Sky was partly cloudy. I told him I will be back after visiting suicide point. It was just about one K.m.away fom our hotel. Suicide point is a beautiful place. It is a dense forest area with tall eucalyptus trees. After walking half a kilometer on the main road we had to walk another half kilometer through the forest to reach a suicidal point.

From the main road we took left turn and started walking towards the famous suicide point. After walking for some time we have come to an old depleted house. She gripped my hand. 'Ajay, you see that old building'?

Maybe there is a ghost inside the house"!. I assured her that there are no ghost inside the house. 'Maya, this is not only a reserved forest area but also a tourist center without permission one can not build houses here. Someone had illegally constructed houses and they had abounded half way through the construction. See, construction materials are still lying around. There were wooden logs, concrete roads, blue metals and sand.

As we kept walking Maya was keeping quiet. Being a poetess she must be cooking up something on her mind...

We walked through eucalyptus tree and reached suicide point. From the cliff top it is three thousand feet below is the ground level. About five kilometers away we could see devils peak. Devils peak is about thousand feet in height and four kilometer wide mountain. Top of the mountain is covered in fog. In the clear sky night it appears as if it touches the sky. I wish you could climb over the peak and touch twinkling stars. Hundreds of years ago it was a huge mountain. Devils peak appeared after one portion of the mountain slided down into the valley. Exposing sold granite rocks in pillar formation. In the full moon night white granite reflects moon light. Changing lights make it interesting pattern. I was observing the play of light and shadow. Maya started reciting her poem...poem was about a virgin girl's first experince with orgasam. It was a simple poem but I liked it very much. I did not say thank you. I held her in my arms and gently kissed her on her lips. She felt very happy...

I could hear sound of vechele passing on the highway. Looking in that direction, I noticed a car taking a turn and coming towards us. It stopped about three hundred feet before us in front of the old house. As they opened car door bust of music filled the air. It was so loud. Car head light was still on. Those youngsters must be enjoining life...

Maya told me it was already late. Yes, she was right. We had already spent about forty minutes at the suicide point. It started drizzling. We have to walk one kilometer to reach our hotel. It was 7.45 PM. We started walking towards our hotel. We walked through the woods under the moonlight. As we walked towards the main road music became loud and clear. I noticed on an SUV with headlights on and it's front door kept opened for music to play around. There were four youngsters around thirty years old sitting in front of the SUV and enjoying their drinks. Must be bachelors having good times. We had to pass through that area to go to a main road. Maya felt uncomfortable. She gripped my left hand and started walking fast. I put my hand on her shoulder and told her to cool down there is no need to get alarmed. I assured her 'Don't worry, those youngsters are enjoying their drinks. Don't bother about them.. .Keep walking...'

As we were about to pass them someone commented that my life Maya makes good lay. Others approved of his comment. I looked over my shoulder in the head light I had seen them clearly. We kept walking without responding to them.

One of the guy invited me for drinks "Machan'! (Local slang used to call brother-in law) 'how about joining for drink"?

'Sorry; friends! I do not drink...' There was a Pajero turbo charger in metallic blue color in the back ground. I casually noticed its registration number TN-10-E-4577. It had Chennai registration number.

We both kept walking towards the main road. I heard them saying "Machan, it must be a figure!' It seems they had too many drinks. One of them came after us. Maya tightened her grip on my hand. He caught her left hand. Maya tried to remove his hand. but he held her hand firmly.

'Come on baby, let's have a drink with us!' he offered his half bottle of whiskey.

'Look, gentlemen! Leave her hand ". I forcibly removed his grip on her hand. She won't drink. And she is not your figure. ..I do not want any trouble. Please leave us alone. You all enjoy your drinks. See you some other time" we moved on...

Other guys joined with him and blocked our way. "Machan, you leave her alone ; we will drop her at your place... First thing in the morning. No harm, we promise! They made their intentions very clear. In the car head light I noticed each one of them clearly. They were aged about thirty to thirty five years old guys. My wife was begging them to spare us alone. It was of no use. One of them tries to grab my wife. Two of the guys started pulling Maya from me. I pushed hard and both of them fell down. I pulled her behind me.

'I told you we do not want any more trouble, you all are creating trouble for us'. PLEASE LEAVE US ALONE! 'I grabbed Maya's hand and we started walking briskly. Someone pushed me from behind and I fell on the ground. Maya pleaded not to harm us. I got up. She went on begging them to leave us alone. One of the guy held her and said 'you stay with us, let him go...' I punched him hard on his face. 'Bastard, how dare you say that? I told you she is my wife NOT YOUR FUCKING FIGURE'! A few more pushing and shoving.... She pleaded not to fight. I told Maya to stay behind me. Now they could not touch Maya..

One of them suggested "how about lifting her"? Maya became startled. She tightened her grip on my hand.

Maya... 'Come on, Let's run... we will make it to the highway...' Which is about five hundred feet away. They moved fast, trying to catch up with us. I heard someone

telling... "We will take on the guy first; the rest is assured…" some on tapped on my shoulder. "He, Dude, she looks irresistible to me'. Holding Maya's hand I turned around.

I…. "So what …?"

He continued... "No harm. We will return her tomorrow. ... First thing in the morning". He assured me.

I... She is not my girlfriend. She is my wife. You guys are drunk. I do not want any more trouble. Just leave us alone".

One of the guy lunged at Maya and caught her hand. "I need her badly". I pushed him hard. Maya pulled out her hand and he fell on the ground. He screamed..." Fix that son of a bitch". Others started closing on us. I moved Maya behind me. I never fought in my life time. The person on the ground got up. Now I have to face four guys. I was able to dodge a few punches and managed to returned couple of punches back to them. It became a free for all. The harder I hit them the more they became violent. Maya pulled me from behind asked me to run…

I... "Maya. Run up to main road and get help and reach the hotel. I will manage these guys". But she would not listen.

Maya… "Ajay. I just can't leave you like that".

As the fight rages on I found myself at the receiving end. This is no scene from the Bollywood movie where skinny hero bash up dozens of thugs or one kick from the hero and bad guys travel through the air and land at the far end of the street. There was no gravity defying fight. Here the fight was not choreographed. It had no rhythm or any synchronized moments. This fight was real and happening in real time...

The big bad guy mouthed few punch dialogs. "Save your life. if needed we will beat you to death". He made his

intentions are very clear. After they beat me to death they will gang rape my wife. I was thinking … Never in my life i had to fight. Why all these things are happing to me? I am a good guy with clean habits. The atheist will pacify his mind by saying..." God will test only good people to check his loyalty. Shit!

I ... "Maya run for your life..." she was too terrified to obey my order.

Near by there were old pine woods were cut and stacked. About four inch thickness and four feet in length logs. one of the guy ordered others to pick up wooden log. I pushed him down and we both started running toward the main road. Someone flung the log. It hits my ankle and I fell down. They caught up with us. As I tried to get up they beat me badly. Maya tried to prevent them. She too was beaten up. I got up and caught hold of one of the log and pulled it hard. The guy at the other end came close to me. I gave him one good heading on his nose. As he fell back with a bloody nose I pulled out log from him.. He screamed at the others.. "Spread around..". they encircled us and started beating with wooden log. Maya hugged me from behind to protect me. She was crying and pleading them to spare my life.

Now there are two guys in front of me and the other two guys are behind me. Maya was very scared and was crying. While two of the guys attacked me from the front with punches and kicks other two guys started man handling Maya. I am no super hero of Hindi films. I could hardly defend two of those guys. While I tried to free Maya from their clutches I revived sever blow on my blow on my back. I really got wild and hit them with bloody force. They started beating me with wooden logs. Maya fell at their feet and begged to spare my life. None of them would listened to her.

I caught hold of one of the log and pulled it real hard towards me. As the guy on the other end came closer to me i gave him bloody heading on his nose. He lost his grip on log and started feeling giddy. Must be counting stars. His nose was bloodied and blood started oozing out of his nose. I swung wooden log with great force and broke his jaw bone. He fell on the ground. Meanwhile three other kept beating me. Maya tries to protect me, she too received beating. It was a bloody mess. I could only concentrate on one guy at a time.

'Maya, i will manage, you run up to the main road and get some help to reach the hotel. Don't worry about me...' But she won't listen to me.

'Ayay, without you I am not gong any where'... i really got angry with her.

I pushed her aside… 'RUN..MAYA...RUN.... After hesitating for a while she started running towards the main road.. ...

Maya …. "I will get you help… take care..."

She began running towards the main road.

I heard Maya screaming for help 'AJAY..." HELP. AJAY....' As I looked over my shoulder I received a bloody blow on the back of my hip. It broke my spine and I fell on my back. I tried to get up, but could I not. The pain was unbearable. They hit me hard on my head. Blood started running over my face. They were systematically breaking every part of my body. In the still of the night I could hear Maya begging for mercy. Someone was forcing on her. She screamed …calling out my name... Every time I tried to get up they beat me to the ground. I was half dead. I could not hear any more of Maya's cry. I was waiting there to die... The other guy left Maya and came back to me... They took the badly injured guy to his SUV. When he returned he had

a concrete steel rod about six feet in length in his hand. He yelled at me "BASTURD, YOU ARE DEAD!...." He sends the concreat rod right through my heart. Without much struggle I died.

Someone brought diesel from the SUV and poured onto the wooden log and lit the fire. They threw me over the fire. Seeing the fire she managed to get up and came back... Only to get gang raped by other guys...

What started as drizzling became rain. By the time those guys finished Maya she was as good as dead. They left the place in an SUV.

After some time Maya regained conscious. She looked around and found my body burning bright. With her bare hands she started removing burning woods to recover my body....

SUV stopped half way and switched off the head lights. One of the guy insisted that they should not leave her alive. No more living proof. One of the guy got out of the SUV as he wallked towards Maya he picked up wooden log. Maya was busy removing burning woods with her bear hands. he came behind Maya and hit her hard with the log. her skull was broken and she fell on the buring woods. He tossed wooden log into the fire and walked towords the SUV. Again it started raining.

He got into the SUV and asked his friend to drive the nearest hospital to give first aid for his injured freind. after driving about twenty minutes the found one privet houspetal on the hight way. They all carried his firend to the hospital. Night duty doctor checked his injured friend.

'He is bady injured, I need to take ex-ray to access the damage to his jaw bone. how did it happend?

"we were all drinking. my friend got drunk. after some time he went for urinal there he slipped and fell of the clif.

his face hit against the tree trunk. later when we went searching for him we found him unconcious under the tree. Give him first aid we wants to take him to chennai city hosptial immideatly".

Doctor belived his story. he took ex-ray and found there was a hairline crack on jaw bone. He then stiched his broken skin and gave collar support for the neck. After paying hospital bill they left for chennai city hospital.

Even in the pouring rain my body burned like a wooden log. Thundering and lighting becomes intense. One of the lightning split into two. One end struck the nearby tree and it was cut into two. The other end struck with the concrete rod. Sending millions of volts throughout my body. I felt my whole body energized. I spread both my arms sending burning woods flying. I got up from the fire. I looked around the place. At first i had thermal vision. Gradually my vision returned normal. I can even see in the dark!

I notice concrete six feet long concret rod sticking out of my heart. I slowly pulled it out of my chest. I felt no pain. After i pulled out blood started pouring out. i looked at myself. my body had charcoal color. Except my heart and lungs my skin, internal organs including my private parts were completely burnt out. Still my heart was beating! Blood was gushing out from my heart and there was a gaping hole in my chest. Through the hole in my rib cage I could see my heart glowing slowly with each heart beat.. Even though the rain had stopped, my body was still burning bright. All my other systems worked better than normal. I think I had aquried super power. I myself is not aware of my own powers!

No more bad guys. No SUV either. Suddenly I remembered Maya.I called out Maya. ... As I came out of

the flame I stumpled and fell on the ground. I took a closer look and found it was Maya's her dead body.

The rain had stopped and the moon emerged from the clouds. Maya was hit hard on her head. Her skull was broken. Her dress was bloodied and covered with mud. I sank to my knees and broke down. I placed her head on my lap and started crying. I do not know how long…

How can life be so cruel to us? Is this what people call it fate? I thought for a while … I cannot carry her body back home. I have to bury her body here… I gently placed her body on the ground..

I have to give her decent burial before I go hunting rapist cum killers. I carried her body in my arms and placed it near a banyan tree. I needed something to dig grave. In the lighting I saw the old abandoned house in the middle of trees. Then I remembered the haunted house. I went there to search for something to dig. I walked towards the house. As I moved closer, I noticed it was not a haunted house but an abounded house half way though the construction. There must be some reason behind it. The main door was not locked. I slightly pushed opened the main door. With a cracking noise door opened into the main hall. I looked around, it was damp and green fungus all over the wall. Plastering was not done. Spider web covered the ceiling. I looked at the center of the ceiling there was a rope hanging from the ceiling at the end of the rope I found a dead man hanging on it. On a closer look, I found it was an old man. He may be one of the construction workers. He might have hanged himself. I wanted to remove his body and place it on the floor. As I tried to touch his body my hand went right through him! However, the body is still hanging there! What does it mean? I can see dead people! The old man had died years ago and his body is no more there! It was like an optical illusion.

Again it started raining. I went back yard and found one old shovel and crow bar. I came back and started digging grave for Maya. It took time to dig grave for her. Once the grave was ready, I lifted Maya's body and gently placed it in the grave. " My poor Maya …she will never come back. May be God had sent me back to avenge those killers..." it was the hardest thing in my life to bury my own wife. I gave her one last gently kissed on her lips "Maya I am sorry I could not save you. Maya... You sleep here... I promise you that I will hunt down and kill each one of them and I will come back to you. Life has been so cruel to us" There were no flowers to cover her body. Even my tears were washed out by rain. I remove my wedding ring and placed it on her finger. After I covered her grave, I prayed for her soul. With heavy heart I was about to move out...

Near by the bush some animal was stealthily moving towards me. In the dark, I noticed two emerald eyes staring at me. Other then eyes I could not see anything. It's body was covered in the bush. Suddenly animal sprang into life and leaped at me... "Holly shit! It was a big black panther. Other then run for life there was no time to react. I tried to dodge panther by running helter skelter. Running at my top speed it was difficult to maneuver thought the pine woods. I did not know that I was running towards the suicide point. Panther tried to tap on my leg twice it missed my leg by whiskers. ...

Few more trees to avoid before I can take off from the cliff. That darned animal was just behind me. If panther takes one giant leap then I will become history. Running zing zag at the top of my speed was not a joke especially when a panther is after my flesh. As I was running I looked over my shoulder, panther was already air born! Suddenly I noticed one huge banyan tree right in front of me! There was no time to maneuver the tree. I just darted through

the tree only to find myself taking off from the cliff. I felt like a feather. I hit the waterfall three thousand feet below. panther smashed his head against the banyan tree and died on the spot. I felt as if I was inside the tumbler washer. Gushing water from the height of three thousand feet washed out my burnt outer skin. Water current took me far away. I managed to climb out of the river.

My pealed off body exposed raw flesh and nerves. When i came out of the waterfall, I noticed not only my burnt skin but also my vital internal organs and privet parts were also gone! Still I am alive! Why? Without outer skin I had a ghastly look. Even I hate myself. The rain had stopped and the moon had emerged from the clouds.

I lay on the nearer by rock and started thinking ... why I am still alive? God had sent me to avenge the killers of my wife. I will hunt down and kill each one of them. I think I had acquired special powers after I was burnt alive...I can see in the dark I had even seen a dead man in the old haunted house who died years ago. I ran right through the banyan tree! What happened to the panther? Poor panther he could not run though the tree... He must have broken his skull against the tree. I always loved animal... May his soul rest in peace...!

I tried to recollect events leading to my death.

We were returning back to our hotel. An SUV with its head lights on with loud music ....four were guys were drinking in front of the SUV. Again I replayed it in my mind. I missed out something....we were returning back to our hotel...... SUV with its light on .... And its registration number is T.N-10-E-4577. A Pajero turbo charger with metallic blue color. The registration belongs to Chennai city. Now I need to find out its owner. It belongs to any one of those guys. Others could be his friends or colleagues. I will find them at any cost...

I lay there for some more time... I got up and started thinking whether to go back to the hotel or go hunting those killers. There is no need to go back to Lake view hotel. After waiting for few days hotel manager will contact my family. I decided not to return back to the hotel.

From there I saw one villager was walking towards me with a big bundle of grass on his head. I have to go to Chennai to hunt down those killers. I walked towards him. I need to ask him direction for the main road. As he came close to me I asked him "Which is the way to main road"?

He said 'what'?! Even though I was standing right in front of him,he looked around to see me. "When is the last bus to Chennai city'? It seems he could not see me. He looked at my shadow on the ground. He then looked at my face. His jaw dropped open. Bundle of fodder fell off his head. He dropped his head load and screamed 'GHOST'!.... 'GHOST'!! And started running for his life. As he ran I saw him falling now and then. Poor villager... It seems I am invisible to him.

It sets me thinking. He was looking at my shadow around my feet. Does that means he can't see me? Yes! It means he can hear me but he can not see me! My voice is intact. Had he seen me with my peeled of the body he would have fainted. That means human being cannot see me. They only can see my shadow. After the reincarnation I am learning bit by bit about my own new ability! I have acquired super powers!! Is it a bane or boon? Only time can tell because I myself is not fully aware of my own unusual powers.

Far from the mountain range I could hear vehicles moving sound. As it came closer I noticed it was a bus. It must be going towards the city. I ran through the woods as the bus was passing below me and jumped on the top of it. I managed to sneak inside the bus. it was half empty. I

settled down at the back seat. It is 514 K.M long journey to Chennai. it will take more than twelve hours to reach chennai. I started planning how to trace out those killers. Soon I fell asleep and slept like a wooden log.

Next day at 8 a.m. When lodge manger Mr.Kumar came for duty security man Mani informed him that the young couple who went for evening walk did not return. He checked their address on the computer and found those young couples are from New Delhi. He tried their mobile number, it kept ringing but there was no response. He got worried about them. They are new to Kodaikanal. They do not know anyone here. Yesterday evening it was raining. Where did they go?

He rang up to his friend Ravi Kumar. He is the inspector at the local police station. He told about the disappearance of a young couple. Ravi Kumar heard everything very carefully. He told Kumar to come to the police station and to give written complaint. Kumar readily agreed to it. He then took duplicate key and went to the first floor of room no 13. He found two of their mobile phones on the dressing table. He locked their room and came back to the reception. He expected his inspector friend to search for the young couple.

Visitors started arriving at the suicide point around 8 am. Some of them noticed burnt out wooden logs near the old building. Others found a grave under the banyan tree.... Local guide found it odd. A grave under the banyan tree! He called up local police station. Inspector Ravi Kumar received the call. After listening, he thanked him. He also asked the local guide to keep visitors off the suicide point.

Ravi Kumar and two other sub inspector visited the place. He asked all the visitors to move out of the place and sealed the area. No visitors beyond this point banner was put on.

There were burned out wooden logs... Tire marking near the old building...... Further down under the banyan tree there is a grave.. ... He ordered sub inspector to bring two helpers to dig up the grave. In about fifteen minutes sub inspectors came back with two helpers. They carefully removed earth with a shovel from the grave. About four feet below they found burnt out body of a female aged around twenty six. The inspector took photographs with his cell phone camera. He observed a few things. It was a burnt body of a young woman with her gold ornaments intact. Her clothes are not completely burnt out. There are two wedding rings on her left ring finger! Where is her husband missing? He asked two of his sub inspectors to search the entire area. But they could not locate her husband or his body. " After killing his young wife did he commit suicide by jumping off the cliff? He decided to wait for the autopsy before coming into conclusion. After writing a detailed report he sent the body to the government hospital for an autopsy and waited for report.

Inspector Ravi Kumar rang up and asked lodge manger Kumar to come to the police station. In about fifteen minutes Kumar arrived at the police station. Inspector showed photographs of the burnt body of a young woman. It did not take much time for Kumar to recognize Maya's body. "It is the same woman who stayed in our lodge with her husband. They are newly married couples. Very much in love. Came here for honeymoon. Where is her husband missing?" he asked inspector Ravi Kumar.

"Kumar, there is no trace of her husband. I am unable to conclude anything at the moment. There are two wedding ring on her left ring finger.. The other wedding ring belongs to her husband. He must have killed her first, then he burnt her body before jumping off the cliff? There is a car tire marking near the old building..... Liquor bottles and half

eaten snaks packets.... Remember yesterday evening after six thirty it was raining. ....lots of vital proof we had lost in the rain... i will have to wait till the autopsy report before I can proceed any further... It will be ready by afternoon...."

"Come with me, you can check their room for any clue...." Kumar invited Ravi Kumar to his lodge.

"Naturally I will have to check their room. It will help for investigation" both of them left for lake view lodge.

Kumar opened the register on a computer. Ajay and Maya photograph with full address was there. He then showed him footage from CCTV. Ajay and Maya had a few words with the manager in the lobby before they moved out of the hotel yesterday evening at 6.p.m.

Ravi Kumar asked for CCTV footage and their photos with detail address. After copying it on his pen drive he thanked Kumar and left for the police station.

Next day at about 8.30 am I woke up and looked through the window. We were somewhere around the suburban area of Chennai city. In about few minutes I had noticed the big arch welcoming us to Chennai city at Marimalai Nagar which is about 45 K.M from the city. It will take another 50 minutes to reach Chennai city bus terminus. If I get down at the Chennai bus terminus it will create lots of problem for the public. First I need to find out the nearest regional transport office (RTO).

Near the city bus terminus bus was waiting for the signal. Few of the shops were opened on the side of the main road. I noticed one of the supermarkets kept opened. As I put my head through the window I noticed my reflection in a rear mirror of near by bus. My real image without skin. Even for me it was horrifying sight. I hate the sight of me. Apart from my shadow my real image can be seen on the reflecting surface of mirror,glass and water. I pulled out my head.

If I walked around the area whole crowd is going to run helter skelter if they see my shadow or my reflection. I leaped out of the window to main High way,vehicles kept passing through me!

I walked towards the nearby supermarket. I saw the sales girl at the cash counter. I pushed opened main glass door and entered into the supermarket. From the corner of sale girl she noticed main door opening automatically. She could not believe her eyes. She kept looking at the main door in astonishment. I walked in front of her towards book section which was on her right side. She dismissed what she had seen. Refusing to acknowledge fact. Automatic door opening and closing can not happen. It must be an illusion. She went on to check balance cash.

From the book shelf I took out city map. Opened it and looked for an important government office address. Places of interest, central and sate govt office address etc. I looked for RTO office. It was there in D-4 section. I found nearest one is in Virugambakkam. Chennai.92. It is about one and half k.m away from here. After finishing counting cash Sales girl once again looked at the main gate. She found nothing unusual. She looked at my direction. I kept the book back into the shelf. She noticed city guide map getting back to its own shelf!. She was shit scared she could not even scream. As I walked towards the main door her eyes followed my shadow. She looked at me and I smiled back! She was watching my reflection on the mirror. It did not notice there was a cosmetic counter just opposite to her counter. She had only seen me for a few second in the flesh. Without even making noise she collapsed in the chair. I opened the main door and came out of the supermarket. Walked across the main high way,vehicles kept passing through me!

The nearest RTO office is in Virugambakkam. I had memorized place and route to virugambakkam RT office. It is just one and half kilometer from bus terminal. But if I go by walk people will notice my shadow image on the street and it will create problem for all of us. There is only one way to avoid it. Travel on top of the vehicle. I waited under the shadow of the building to take vichale me to virugambakkam. Soon I found vechile taking a right turn and going towards virugambakkam. I ran and jumped on top of the car. At the virugambakkam I jumped on top of the vehicle going towards Alwarthirunagar. RT office is inside the Alwarthirunagar colony just four buildings away from the main road.

I had jumped out of vehile at Alwarthiru Nagar. Someone took note of my moving shadow image. Among the crowd, someone pointed at my shadow and screamed "Ghost"! Look there is a ghost moving around". Others asked in unison. "Where...? Where...? They all wanted to see me. if they see me in flesh few of them will get pissed off! Perhaps people are seeing ghost for the first time in daylight.

It is common in Indian cities, you will find stray dogs in most of the places. There were about four of them. it seems dog can see me. They moved closer to me and started howling and barking at me. People waiting for the bus at the bus stop looked at my direction. vechale kept passing by me. One of the dog came close to bite me. I gave him bloody kick it fell on the other side of the road. it got up and run for his life. The rest of the dogs ran away. Keeping a safe distance dogs kept on barking at me.

People at the bus stop noticed a shadow image of me on the roadside. Some of them with cell phone took moving shadow of my image. Few of them reported to T.V and F.M station. I did not waste my time. I crossed over

the road 'through the passing vehicle! Even after coming other side of the road people kept looking on the opposite side of the road!. I walked into Alwarthiru Nagar colony. There were trees on either side of the footpath. Now my own shadow is not visible on the ground. I found RToffice on my right it was the fourth building from the main road. RT office was locked. The government office in Indian will open only after 10 a.m. I was too early, people are yet to come to office.

At first I thought of breaking the main door lock with stone. Then I remembered running through the banyan tree at Kodikanal to save my life from black panther. I walked through the main door. it was not a paperless office. On the rack there were record books,ledgers and files.

I switched on the computer. Password....? Being a software engineer and ethical hacker it was not a big deal for me. After retrieving the password from the computer I logged in RTOCHI92. It was a short form of Regional Transport office Chennai. Pin code 92. On search I had typed vehicle number. TN-10-E-4577 and waited for the result.........

File opened up.

A2005 - 0140219

GOVERMENT OF TAMIL NADU.

TRASPORT DEPARTMENT.

TA-05

AA-1957

CERTIFICATE OF REGISTRATION.

Registration No: T.N.10-E-4577

Discription of Vechicle : PAJIRO turbo charger.

Name of Registered Owner. Raj Kumar.

Full Address NAME : Raj Kumar; plot No: 1957, House

No:13-A. Third main road, Mahalaxmi colony, Baasanth Nagar, Chennai-600090.

Makers : Mitshubishi Motors. Japan.

Month & Year of Manufacture.........2005

Number of Cylinders: 4.

Chassis Number: O4BM42C01957.

Engine Number: O4BM4405791

Fuel Used in Engine: Petrol.

Hosre Power (BHP) :1120.

Colour: Metaic Blue.

Date: 15-01-2005

I had to cross check with ledger N0:52. It was on fourth rack. Same address and details of the vehicle were there. The vehicle number it belongs to Raj Kumar, others could be his friends..... Before closing the computer I checked with google map to find out rout to the Basnth Nagar third street. Basant Nagar is about 19 k.m away from Alawar thru Nagar. I closed the file and switched off the computer and came out of the office. I waited under the shadow of the tree for passing vechicle. People walked few feet away from me. After some times I notice cars coming out to the colony. I jumped on top of the car which was heading toward the city. At Vadapalani I noticed 5E bus was running behind the car. I was not sure whether the driver had noticed me my shadow image on top of the car. I took one giant back somersault in the air and landed on top of the bus. Bus E5 will take me directly to Basanth Nagar. I do not have to zig zag across the city by hopping from one vehicle to another vehicle.

At the vadpalani junction bus stopped for signal. Near the shop, I saw people gathered around the T.V.showroom. At first I thought they were watching cricket. I looked at the

T.V and found my own shadow in it! Flash news was on. Breaking news in big bold letters. GHOST IN CHENNAI CITY! It was reported from Virugambakkam. I am here on earth to accomplish my mission....to hunt down and kill four of those killers.

I laid on top of the bus. After about one hour journey bus was entering into the Bus terminus. I did not want to create panic among the public. I only wanted to carry out mission and reach home in New Delhi. The tree was too close to me. I hung on to the branch.

Basanth Nagar was the beautiful nagar. there were with full of trees on either side of the footpath. I walked under the shadow of the tree. When I see some one coming in my direction, I make sure I am under the shadow, if not I will wait for him / her to pass before I come from under the sunlight. I did not want to scare public nor I want ed unwanted attention from the public.

It was Sunday there were not much traffic on the street. I went searching for the address.

Raj Kumar; plot No: 1957, House No:13-A. Third main road, Mahalaxmi colony, Basanth Nagar, Chennai-600090.

After walking abut thirty minutes I found one big house. House tallied with the RT office address. I pushed open the main gate and kept it open. The first thing I noticed was a Pajiro SUV with blue metallic color with same registration number on his portico. I climbed a few steps and was about to press the calling bell. 'Let it be a pleasant surprise' for him. I walked through the main door and entered into the sitting room. There was a family photograph inside the showcase. It's him! His wife and seven years old son was with them. There was no sign of life inside the house. May be because of Sunday, his wife and son would have gone to temple or supermarket. Before

they return back I should kidnap him. I want to move him into secured place. I went into their kitchen and took chopper knife and went to ground floor bedroom. It was empty. I climbed through the staircase and came to the main hall on the first floor. I opened one of the bedroom doors. His son was sleeping with A/C on. I slowly closed the door and went and checked other bedroom. It was a master bedroom. Raj kumar was peacefully sleeping with heavy bandages on his jaw.I locked the bedroom behind me. Keeping chopper knife in my right hand I took jag full of water from the small fridge. I climbed on his master bed and started pouring cold water on his face. Suddenly he opened his eyes. Startled. He stared at the pouring jug. He saw jag automatically pouring water on his face! He screamed GHOST. ..! GHOST...!! he tried to get out of the bed. Kneeling beside him I caught hold of his neck. I was coming 'Alive'....'from my finger tip my body was coming into his view gradually. A peeled off the body of my image. With fear he could not even scream.

I . . 'Remember me? After some time he managed to ask 'who are you....?

I. .. You and your friends killed me and my wife yesterday at the Kodikanal suicide point.

Raj Kumar. ...NO, I did not kill you.... '

I. ..One bloody punch on your jaw you will stop lying. I raised chopper knife pretented him to kill'. I will slaughter you like a goat'.

Raj Kumar....'Yes, my friends told me that they killed you and your wife and set on fire. Now you have come back to kill all of us....?"

I. ... 'Yes, I will hunt down each one of you and kill just the way you killed me and my wife. Now none of you can do anything to me. I had acquired super natural power. Nothing can stop me till I finish all of you....'

Raj Kumar...plz, I am a family man, I did not kill you or your wife. You know that very well. You broke my jaw with one bloody blow and I fell unconscious. Please spare me and my family. I beg you...'

I... I will spare you and your family only on one condition. I know you did not kill me or my wife. You have to co-operate with me.......... You are coming with me to a secret place and stay there. I do not want you to alert your friends nor I want them to escape from me. Once I finished all those bastards I will come and set you free.. If you do not cooperate I am going to kill you here on your bed. . ..' I place knife on his throth. With you or without you I am going to kill each one of them..' That was a lie. And your life goes waste. .'

Raj Kumar. 'Don't kill me....If you spare me and my family I will come with you...'

I. ... 'Good, Now take car key, just follow my instructions and you will be safe' I allowed him to get up. He took SUV key and we got into it. I sat behind him with chopper knife.

Raj Kumar. 'Where are we going'?

I 'Go to East coast road, just after the Muthukadu lake there is an old building. You will stay there till I come back in a matter of hours. Then I will set you free...'

It took about forty five minutes from Basant Nagar to reach Muthukadu. After the lake bridge I asked him to take the right turn road along the lake. At the far end of the road there was a depleted building. I pulled out the car key and we both got out of the car. After climbing through the steps we came to first floor.

I 'I want three of your friends detailed address. If the address is wrong or if I can not find them in their address I will come back and kill you.. No mercy' I warned him.

Raj Kumar. ..'They are my business partners in building construction company. I will give you complete address. You spare my family that is all I am asking you...."

I 'O.K, Now tell me their address I can remember'.

Raj Kumar. 'Kathik, he is staying at Anna Nagar.

I "I want detail address'

Raj Kumar 'Karthik, Plot No: 29/2, House No 132, Block AZ. Second cross street; Anna Nagar East. Chennai-102.

I 'Next?

Raj Kumar 'Arun. Staying at Adyar boat club area. RA Puram. Plot No.196, House No. 33, boat club road. R.A. Puram. Chennai-600033.

I 'Who is the third guy'?

Raj Kumar 'Rajesh. He is staying at Sky walk apartment. it is the tallest building in Chennai, 32 floors. It is near the East coast road on the beach front. He is financing our housing project. He is very rich, staying tallest building on ECR; Skywalk apartment on 30 th floor. D. Block. Flat no 4. Door No. 13. East coast road. Chennai-101.

I got all their address. These guys should not run away. Raj Kumar should not inform them about my mission. I looked around the room and found ropes.. 'Till I came back you should not run away. . or you are going to inform about my plans to your friends. I am going to tie you..... when I came back I will set you free...' he was shit scared of me. ..I know he will not take chances with me.... He is now at my mercy. I tied his hands behind him and also his both legs. i took the car key and got into it.

Kathik first.

Anna Nagar is far away from Muthukadu lake area. I came back to city via old Mahbali Puram road (OMR). Anna Nagar is the biggest colony in Tamil Nadu. I went to

the Anna Nagar tower. It is a landmark area in Anna Nagar. There I found the layout of Anna Nagar. I slightly lowered the windshield and looked for AZ block; plot No; 29/2A,. It was fourth left on second street. I shifted gears...

On the second street I searched for House No: 132. It is the fifth house from the right side. I parked SUV ahead of the house and waited for people to pass by the car. When no one was around the place I opened the door and got out of the SUV. There was a metallic gate about six feet tall. I jumped over the gate and went straight through the main door. Once inside the sitting room I looked around the place. It was a bloody mess. He must be a bachelor. It was already 2 p.m. No one was on the ground floor. I went upstairs. His bedroom was not locked. I opened the door and went inside. He already had a few drinks from the bottle and was sleeping. I closed the door behind me and sat on a chair. I was thinking how to kill him. If I kill him in his sleep he will not know who killed him and why I had to kill him. I have to wake him up so that he will understand why I wanted to kill him.

I got up from the chair and took the liquor bottle and threw it against the wall. Hearing the bottle breaking noise he woke up. He looked at the broken bottle.

"I am here to kill you...."startled he got up from the bed. He looked in my direction and switched on the table lamp. Seeing my shadow image on the wall he got scared. He got out of the bed.

"Who are you? And why do you want to kill me?"

"You and your friends raped my wife and killed both of us yesterday night at Kodaikanal suicide point. Now you remember me?"

He wiped out his sweat from his forehead. As I moved closer to him he walked backwards. The wall stopped him walking further back. He searched for something to

hit me. I caught him by his neck with my left hand.... I started 'coming alive'. With my right hand I punched his face real hard repeatedly. His face became bloodied. He started chocking. Side of the bed table there were apples and knife on a silver plate. He grabbed a knife and plunged into my left arm shoulder muscle. It was bloody painful. Blood started dripping onto the floor. I pushed him back and started moving backwards. Seeing blood dripping on the floor and my moving image he repeatedly knifed me. I could feel knife moving through my body. I gradually disappeared in front of his eyes. I pushed him hard and he fell on the floor next to the bed. He took out a gun from under the bed and got up.

He came forward and pointed gun at my head! "BASTURD, YOU ARE DEAD'! He fired twice. Bullets went right through my head! Standing right in front of him I noticed he was not looking at me but my reflection in the mirror which was behind me on the wall. In the mirror image he could see me in the flesh. He looked terrified. His hand was shakings nether the less he fired right through my head twice. I could hear broken mirror falling onto the floor. When I looked over my shoulder I noticed I was standing right in front of a huge wall mirror. With my left hand I caught hold of his hand. I was gradually coming into his view. I forcibly kept me away from his firing line. He fired two more bullets in rapid session. In desperation he wasted two more bullets. Right in front of him I am very much "alive and kicking". You must see the horror on his face. I gave him a bloody blow on his face as he kept falling he kept firing at me.. ..I could feel the bullets passing through me. He had emptied his gun.....he tried to escape by running towards the bedroom door. I was double fast. I kicked in his left leg and he fell flat on the floor. I lifted him and threw him against the wall. He landed on his head

and broke his neck. I lifted the wooden chair to hit him. He begged me to spare his life. "Please don't kill me.... I beg you...please...." I dropped the chair.

"My wife begged you all to spare our lives. in return you all raped my wife and killed both of us. I came back to life but my wife will never ever come back to life. God had sent me to kill you all.... After I kill you I will kill your friends Arun and Rajesh. You lesser mortals can do nothing to stop me. .." as I moved out of the room he kept track of my shadow image. Having broken his neck he could not move out of the bedroom

I came to the main hall. There are two other bedroom on the first floor.I could not find anything to kill him. At the far end there was a small pantry room. There was a fridge and gas stove with few vessels. I closed gas cylinder knob and removed rubber hose connection and carried cylinder to his bedroom and closed bedroom door behind me. I opened a gas cylinder regulator knob. Gushing gash made a hissing noise. He went on with his pleading....room was getting filled with gas pretty fast. I moved to words bedside table. My shadow image is the only clue for him to follow my movements. I took out his antique table lamp made out of marble and switched on. He again begged me... "Please don't kill me…."

YOU, BASTURD! YOU ARE DEAD NOW!!' I Smashed lamp against the wall. 'Table lamp broken into several pieces and there was the spark which ignited the gas. The entire room was engulfed in flame. Even my body burnt brightly.Screaming frantically and moved like a snake through the floor. As I walked towards the bedroom door I looked over my shoulder. His body was on fire. He cried for help.... As I walked through the bedroom door he looked at me with astonishment. I had hardly moved couples of the steps cylinder blast had sent me right across the garden.

Front portion of the first floor was blown away. I landed near the main gate. Hearing the blast sound people from the main road pushed opened the main gate and "ran through' me to save him. I moved under the tree shadow and walked towards the SUV. I got into the SUV and zoomed out of the scene.

Next target. ARUN.

I know boat club is in RA Puram near the park Sheraton hotel. I went searching for the address. After searching for about thirty five minutes I was able to locate his house. I parked SUV away from his house and walked under the tree shadow. Seeing my shadow image on the street I do not want any one trailing me. I am already on the air (T.V) my shadow image at virugambakkam is still being played on almost every T.V channels and all over the world and net. I had even noticed people gathering around T.V selling shops. Since it was Sunday there were hardly any traffic or people around the place. I had noticed only few passing vehicles.

I jumped over the gate and walked towards his house. Suddenly I saw Arun coming out of his house neatly dressed. He is about to go out. I hide behind his car. He locked his house and unlocked his car door with his remote key and went to the main gate and kept it open. Meanwhile I got into his car and sat behind the driver's seat. I had turned the rear mirror towards left side. He got into the car and switched on the music system. Loud heavy metallic music came alive. He stopped by the roadside and went to lock the main gate with a chain and lock. He started the car and drove towards the Adyar area. I had no idea where he was going.......

Even though it was raining outside he switched on A/C. He enjoyed fast music with strobe lights. We were heading towards Adayar. Is he going to meet his friend Raj Kumar at

Basent Nagar? I had to wait and see. When the green signal turned on instead of taking left he went straight on the main road. Now we are heading towards Eeat coast road. Perhaps he is going to meet his friend Rajesh at Skywalk apartments.

After some time I noticed Skywalk apartments on the beach front from the east coast road. It was thirty two stories tallest buildings. It had four blocks. He drove straight. The car went cruising along the east coast road. ... He must be heading towards Kovalam or Mahablaipiram beach resort. After about thirty minutes of running time we were heading towards the Muthukadu lake bridge. A long distance bus was trying to overtake our car. Diver kept pressing the horn.. He looked at the rear mirror. It was tilted towards left. He gave way to the bus and he adjusted the mirror. I gave him warm smiled. Seeing my reflection on the mirror he got pissed off! The car went out of control for a few seconds but he managed to control. I looked road ahead. I could see the Muthu Kadu bridge at the far end. We were approaching pretty fast. Inside the A/C car he was sweating profusely.

I ... "Do you remember me"?

Arun " who are you"? Ghost? What do you want"?

I. . "You burnt me alive at KodaiKanal. I am going to take of your life out"

We were about to enter the MuthuKadu bride. I put both hands around his neck and strangled him. He kept one hand on the steering wheel and try to remove my hand with his left hand. I tightened my grip on his neck and tried to pull him back seat. He started choking. He removed his right and from the steering wheel. With both hands he tried to remove my grip on his neck. The car went out of control and started running parallel to the main road. As he struggled to release my grip on his throat, instead of

slamming on the break he stepped on the accelerator!. .... 100 k. M.....120 k. M.......150 k.m. .... Car plunged into the Muthukadu lake.

After the car plunged into the lake. He unbuckled seat belt. As soon as he removed his seat belt, I pulled him over the seat. While struggling free from me he kicked on the windshield and it came off. In a few seconds the car was flooded with lake water. I pulled him to back seat. He struggled to free my grip around his neck. I had a vice like grip on his neck. He struggled for some time for his life. I strangulated him with my bare hands. He struggled a lot before he died in front of my eyes. I had the satisfaction of killing him tenderly. Before I moved out of the car I made sure he was dead once for all. I swam out of the car and came to surface. I noticed people taking photos and video with their mobile phone. Few of them were talking over their cell phone. I swam under the water and reached under the bridge. I felt very tired and laid under the bridge for sometimes.

Meanwhile at Kodikanal police station inspector Ravi Kumar received the autopsy report in the evening.

Autopsy report.

There is a very clear evidence that the young woman was gang raped first. Due to heavy blow to her head with a wooden log or stone she died instantaneously. Part of her skull was broken at the back of her head. Later they (rapist cum killers) burnt her body to avoid evidence.....

Autopsy report sets him thinking..... So, there is a connection with car tires. There are more than two people involved in rape cum murder case. These guys beat up her husband and gang raped her. Later they killed her and burnt her body.. .. Did they kill her husband too? Where is her husband ? Where is his body missing? Perhaps they killed him too and threw his body from suicide point.

Ground level is more than three thousand below..... It is a reserved forest area.... Retrieving his body is not easy... Wild animal could have eaten up his body..... Yesterday's rain had wiped out all the vital clues to arrest the culprits...there is no eyewitness in this case..... Now finding out those rapist cum murders is not easy......

First some privet T.V crew members arrived on the banks of Muthukadu lake they went around shooting accident place. A young teenage girl went around the small crowd and asked the witness about the accident. Few of them replied to her. She then went on giving a detailed account of the incident. Side show was going on.....

After some times I heard police vehicle siren followed by the fire service. Lots of people gathered around the cliff. Divers from the fire service jumped into the lake for search and rescue mission. In about twenty minutes a huge crane was pressed into service. They lifted the car out of the lake. Too many people gathered around the car and I could not see what was happening from my point of view. An ambulance took the Rajesh body to a government hospital. Car was towed to the nearest police station. Gradually people started moving out of the place. I was planning for my final mission. I spent more than two hours there. It was already 7 p.m.

Next target. Rajesh.

It is time to act. I came from under the lake bridge. If I returned to the same road I can get down at the sky line apartment. At 7 p.m. The Muthukadu lake area looks like deserted place. All the people from the lake area had already left for their home. Being Sunday very few vehicles were playing on the road. After waiting for about thirty minutes I saw a car fast heading towards the city. As it reached close to me I jumped on top of it. In about forty minutes I landed in front of skyline apartment.

It was around 7.45 PM. Sky line was a gated residential complex. It was thirty two storied flats. Tallest in Tamil Nadu. I made a few observations around the place. Most of the people were busy watching T.V movies. Few old people were sitting under a lamp and were chatting in their park. Some of the were walking around the park. Only one security guard was on duty. He was inside the security office reading local magazine. After standing under the shadow of a tree I made my move very carefully and reached block-B ground floor. I do not want to anyone to see my presence, my shadow image on the floor or on the walls. Whenever I heard people coming on my way I hide behind the concrete pillar of the building. Carefully I made it to the block - D and checked his address on the board. NAME. Rajesh, Skywalk Apartment. 30 th floor, D-Block, Door No. 13.... I got into thc lift and reached 30th floor.

The main door was locked. I walked through the main door and entered into their sitting room cum dining room. The first thing I noticed was a garlanded photo of his mother. It was a luxury house. One corner of the room there was a small pub with foreign liquors. Sitting room had decorated rose wooden partition for the dinning room. I took out their family album from the showcase. His father is a business man. That means he and his father is staying in the house. After inspecting his house I came and settle down in the visiting room.

There was a remote control on the tea poi but no T.V. I looked around and found projection T.V mounted on the opposite wall. I switched on the T.V. With room light clarity was not good I went and switched off the main light and settled on the sofa and waited for him.

After about fifteen minutes I heard the noise ; someone was trying to open main door with key. Immediately I switched off projection T.V and quickly moved behind the

wooden partition. He opened the main door and switched on the main light. It was Rajesh. He slammed the main door behind him. He took the remote and switched on projection T.V. 9 p.m. The news was on. They were replaying same old news. Breaking news! Ghost in Chennai city! My shadow image from Alwar Thiru Nagar......... Cylinder blast at Anna Nagar with Karthik's photo in one corner........., Car fished out of the Muthu Kadu lake with Arun's photo. ..... The news reader was trying to say that it was the handy work of a ghost!

Seeing his friend's horrible death Rajesh started crying. I came to sitting room and walked in front of the big screen. Seeing my shadow image he got scared. I stopped and looked at him.

"I killed two of your friends, Now it is your turn!" and started walking towards him. Seeing my shadow image approaching him he got up and tried to run away. I pushed him back on the sofa and caught hold of his neck and I started punching his face. Gradually I was coming alive.... Seeing me coming alive he got frightened nevertheless he used both hands to free my grip on his neck and kicked me out of the sofa. I fell onto the carpet floor. He jumped over the sofa and ran out of his house. He ran towards the lift.

How far he is going to run away? I got up and came out of the house. I saw him desperately pressing for lift. As I walked towards him he noticed my moving shadow image on the floor. He did not waste time. He ran through the stairs to the terrace. As he ran toward the terrace he banged on few doors screaming GHOST. ..GHOST. ... He ran through the stairs to the terrace. Hearing the commotion people followed him. . I was not in a hurry. I know I can kill him any time. He sure is no match for me.

Few of them asked him "Rajesh.. What is happening?.

Rajesh… "There is a ghost. He is trying to kill me… he is after my blood..."

Others asked in unison.. where is the ghost? Everybody wants to see me.. I am sure some of them will get pissed off after seeing me..

It was a full moon day. They put on the entire terrace light to see me.

When I entered the terrace he was facing the crowd. I walked through the crowed. To show my presence I moved against the light. My shadow on the over head wall made few of them scream and faint.

As I kept walking toward Raja he kept walking backward. It was a newly constructed apartment. There were unused building materials kept on the terrace. He took out one inch concrete steel rod of five foot length. Judging my distance he swung the concert rod with full force. Rod went right though my body. I felt like a whiff of air. Frantically he tried to hit me. few more times he tried to hit me but it was no use. People were watching us in disbelief. After some time he gave up. He was pretty fast climbing ladder of the overhead water tank. Once on the top he shouted for help.. "DADDY, HELP ME.. SAVE ME DADDY…"

His father had just returned after his duty. He went around the house. He sensed something was terrible wrong. He could hear his son crying for his help. He picked up his service revolver form his room and came running to terrace. I climbed the vertical wall of the huge water tank. Rajesh was looking for my presence, seeming my shadow approaching him he moved towards the corner of the water tank. He again shouted for help.. "DADDY HELP ME…. GHOST IS TRYING TO KILL ME.."

Holding his gun above his head his Dad came out of the crowd and fired two warning shots.. Hearing the gun shot, I looked down and saw his dad. Four more bullets

left. Rajesh was almost corned by me. As he tried to swing the steel rod with great force I caught hold of his wrist with my left hand. I was "alive" now in blood and flesh. This is the time I am most vulnerable. I pulled him towards me with great force as he came close to me I gave him a bloody heading on his nose. His nose was bleeding profusely.. He dropped the rod down and covered his nose with his hand. I took the concrete rod in my hand. His father reached on the water tank top and fired at me but he missed his target. I send concert rod right through Rajesh's heart. He was writhing in pain. I heard one more firing shot. Too bad his dad must have aimed at my head but the bullet went right through Raja's forehead. Two other bullets hit my shoulder As he fell off from the fencing he grabbed me. We both went falling from the top of the thirty two story building. As we kept falling we were rolling in the air. Rajesh hit three phase link wire of the transformer. As soon as he came into contact with live wire his body acted as a fuse. His body was cut into two pieces and fell off the wire. Then my body came into contact with live wire. I felt heavy current passing through my body for few second before 1200 Amps fuse blew up. I remember the loud blast of fuse….. The entire building plunged into darkens. I lay there for some time before I regained my consciousness. When I opened my eyes I saw people in the apartment gathered around the transformer.

"I am alive! Mum, I will be home…." I jumped off the transformer and others followed my shadow till the main road.

I did not bother to go back to Muthukadu to free Raj Kumar. I came to a main road and jumped on top of moving car which was headding towards the city. The car went up to Tripilcane area. It is the one of the densely populated areas in the city. Without making my presence felt I have

to go to Chennai central railway station. Jumping from one moving vehicle to another,I had to travel on top of too many vehicles before I could land on waltex road. waltex road run parallel to the Chennai railway station. I cannot walk through the main gate without disturbing public. I had to climb over the station wall. There were trains waiting to leave for its destination. On the sixth platform train bound for New Delhi was waiting for the signal. The few more minute train will start its journey. From the top of the train I peeped inside the compartment. Not all the compartment were full. I noticed passengers were getting into the A/C sleeper compartment. I 'slid' into the compartment and 'walked through them! I found one of the empty upper berths and settled down for a long journey.. .. It will take more than twenty four hours before it reaches new Delhi. I felt very tired and slept throughout the journey.....

Meanwhile at the muthukadu lake house, after a day's hard work beggers, pretty thief and drug peddlers started arriving. Hearing the cry for help they ran upstairs and found a man tied with ropes. They freed him immediately. Raj Kumar told them some unknown people had hijacked his car and kidnaped him at knife point and tried him with rope and dumped him here. After thanking everyone he came to a main road and got a lift. He arrived at this house around 10.30 p.m.

His wife was very much worried. Since morning she had inquired with all their relatives and friends. Nobody had seen Raj Kumar after she left for the supermarket. She was about to report to the nearest police station. He had never gone anywhere without informing her. Even if it is for business purpose.

Raj Kumar asked his wife to promise not to tell anyone about his disappearance. He told her he was kidnapped at knife point from his bed by a ghost! She could not believe

him. A ghost kidnaped her husband at knife point! What for ? He told her not to cross question him, just to listen and keep it as secret. She remembered T.V news about the presence of ghost in Chennai city. But why should ghost kidnap her husband? If so what is the motivation?

She also remembered her husband's friend and business partner died in gas cylinder blast at an Anne Nagar house. She told him about his friend's unnatural death. Raj Kumar fell silent for some time then he continued. Whatever had happened, I had seen real ghost. He is real.... He can come alive at times! He got supernatural powers. I had experienced it. I am safe. I do not want you to report to the police station. Nobody can do anything to him. I am already scared of him. I do not want him to come back had endanger our life. Let's forget the whole incident. Our family is more important than finding ghost or punishing him. He went and switched on T.V. The channel was till showing a shadow image of the ghost of the Alwar Thiru Nagar area. Cylinder blast site at Anna Nagar. His friends photographs were shown on T.V. One car was fished out of the MuthuKadu lake with his friend Arun's photograph in it. And report from skyline apartment about ghost killing another person called Rajesh. He was totally upset. One of his friends and two of his businesses associated killed by ghost. His wife knew only his fiend not his business associates. He said he is going to take a bath. His wife went and arranged dinner for him. He felt very tired and hungry.

After the bath and dinner he said he is going to sleep. His wife did not want to disturb him. He tried to sleep but could not sleep. ghost was right. He killed three of this business partners. Now I do not have to answer anyone. I am the Boss of ANZ construction company......

I slept like a wooden log inside the A/C sleeper couch.

Next day, around 11 p.m. Train waited on the outer berth for the signal to enter platform No 2. I opened the door and jumped out of the train and climped over the compound wall. Waited under the tree shadow for passing car. In about fifteen minutes I found one car and jumped over it. After passing over several cars I reached my house. I walked though the door and went to my mother's room.

'Maa.... 'She heard my voice and opened her eyes. She looked around but she could not see me. She switched on the table lamp.

'Maa... It's me Ajay........ Standing right in front of you... Seeing my shadow on the wall she fainted onto the bed. I took water from the glass and sprinkled on her face. She opened her eyes and looked very scared.

I. ..Maa, don't scream. I am your son Ajay.. .. I am very much alive.. .. You can see my presence, my shadow but you cannot stand the sight of me. I look horrible.

Maa.... Ajay, I am your mother. I want you to see me alive.

I. ... Maa, you will be scared. When I touch your hand I will come alive. Don't be scared. I was brutally beaten to death and they burned me alive.. ..' my mother stretched her hand.

I.... Maa, close your eyes now.... She closed her eyes. Tears rolled out of her eyes.

I placed my hand on her hand. Gradually I started coming alive. I hugged my mother and started crying.... Blood stated oozing our of my eyes and it fell on her sari.

Maa.... Don't cry Ajay...." I could feel her warm tears on the shoulder. " I am happy to see you alive". She gradually opened her eyes. She first saw my peeled off shoulder. She was no more scared of me.. At least her son was alive. My mum asked about Maya. I had narrated the whole incident.

.... Other than crying what can a mother do.. Poor Maa...

The next day morning phone kept ringing at about 8.am.I was sleeping in my room. Maa was busy preparing brake fast in the kitchen. I got up, went and checked the caller ID number it had KodaiKanal telephone code number. Police must have recovered my home number from my mobile. I rushed to the kitchen. I told my Maa that there is a call from KodaiKanal. .. May be from the lodge manager if not it is from the Kodikanal police station. "Maa.... Do not say that I am here...... Let the police search for me.... You have to speak to them... I will switch on speaker phone...."

Maa came to sitting room. I pressed speaker phone..

"Hello..."

"Could I speak to Ajay...? "

"I am the Ajay's mother speaking.... Ajay is not here. He had gone for honeymoon with his wife. He will be back after one week. I will give you his mobile number you can speak to him. His number is 90001-87654. By the way who is speaking?"

"I am inspector Ravi Kumar from Kodikanal police station. Madam I am sorry to inform you... " He hesitated for a moment. "You son Ajay is missing from his lodge. His wife Maya's body was found near the suicide point" we have confirmed it was Maya with available evidence.... We want you to verify it with you.... So that you can collect her body from the government mortuary. ... Please come at the earliest....

"When it happened?..... How did it happen ?. .... Where is Ajay now? "

"We are still searching for Ajay. Yesterday evening after 6 PM Both of them left their lodge for a causal evening walk. They did not return back. In the morning security

man informed lodge manager.. .. Later I received a phone call from a local guide about the body of a young woman near the suicide point. After verifying with all the available records and CCTV footage we found out that body belongs to Maya....even autopsy report is here with us. Please come to the Kodikanal police station.... I hope we will be able to find out Ajay very soon..."

"OK, Inspector Ravi Kumar I will come with Maya's parents..."

"Thank you... Madam. The line went dead.

"Maa I will not be able to come with you to collect Maya's body. I will stay here. You go to Maya's house and inform them. Do not tell them that I am here. Tell them Ajay is missing from Kodikanal and police is searching for him. They found the only Maya's body near the park. Go to the Kodikanal police station with Maya's parents. Give a written complaint about Ajay's disappearance..... Receive Maya's body and come back. Let the police search for me or my body... Now go to Maya's house. ..... Do not worry about me. Lock the house from outside. .... Never ever say anything about me to anyone.. .. I am just missing nothing else..." she hugged me and cried.

My mother changed her clothes and locked our house from outside. She went straight to Maya's house. Here parents were heartbroken after hearing the news.

My mother and her parents took first available flight to Madurai. From there they took privet taxi and went to the Kodikanal police station..... Maa gives inspector Ravi Kumar a written complaint about my disappearance. From the government mortuary they collected Maya's body. Maya's father went to lodge and met the manager. He handed over our belongings to Maya's father. By evening flight they brought Maya's body back home in New Delhi.

I felt very miserable. I could not attend Maya's funeral. The entire colony people gathered to see her final journey. It could have been very hard for them. She was born and brought up in the same house.. As per our religious right her body buried in the nearby burial ground.

I visited Maya late at night at the burial ground. Her spirit came out of the tomb. We hugged and cried.....

THE END

About the Author

About me... I am a story concept writer. I have written novels and fictions. My ability is to write realistic fictions in different genre. Life/story, family fiction, Sci-Fi, Romantic/ Action/ Thriller, Political Thriller, lesbian love, erotic, pure porn, horror/Thriller and also about a new religion! UNIVERSAL LOVE. The New Religion!

To read all my fiction and article Plz visit my blog
http://jivadax.blogspot.in/